I Believe in Unicorns

Books by the same author

Half a Man

Homecoming

The Kites Are Flying!

Meeting Cézanne

The Mozart Question

My Father Is a Polar Bear

This Morning I Met a Whale

Beowulf

Hansel and Gretel

The Pied Piper of Hamelin

Singing for Mrs Pettigrew

Sir Gawain and the Green Knight

I Believe in Unicorns

Michael Morpurgo

illustrated by
Gary Blythe

WALKER
BOOKS

First published 2005 by
Walker Books Ltd, 87 Vauxhall Walk, London SE11 5HJ

This edition published 2015

2 4 6 8 10 9 7 5 3

Text © 2005 Michael Morpurgo
Illustrations © 2005 Gary Blythe

The right of Michael Morpurgo and Gary Blythe to be identified
as author and illustrator respectively of this work has been asserted by them
in accordance with the Copyright, Designs and Patents Act 1988

This book has been typeset in Adobe Caslon

Printed and bound in Great Britain by Clays Ltd, St Ives plc

British Library Cataloguing in Publication Data:
a catalogue record for this book is available from the British Library

ISBN 978-1-4063-6640-2

www.walker.co.uk

For my grandsons,
Alan and Laurence
M.M.

My name is Tomas Porec.
I was just eight years old when
I first saw the unicorn, and
that was twenty long years ago.

I grew up and live to this day in a mountain village that we like to think is just about big enough to call itself a small town. Hidden away in a remote valley it might seem to travellers passing through that it is far too sleepy for anything of any significance ever to have happened here. Not so, for something

very significant did happen, something both dreadful and wonderful at the same time.

For me as a child this place was my whole world, a place full of familiar wonders. Being an only child I spent a lot of time wandering about on my own. I knew every cobbled alleyway, every lamppost. I knew all the houses, and I knew everyone who lived in them, too – and their dogs. And they knew me. From my bedroom window in the farmhouse where we lived on the edge of town, I could look out over the rooftops to the church tower. I loved to watch the swifts screaming around it in swooping squadrons on summer evenings. I loved the deep dong of the church bell that lingered long in the air. But as for going to church, that was a different matter. If ever I could get out of it I most certainly would. I'd far rather go fishing with Father. He didn't like church any more than I did. Mother and Grandma always went, religiously.

But church or not, Sunday was always the best day of the week. In the cold of winter Father and I would go tobogganing on the hillside. In the heat of the summer we'd swim in the lakes and stand there under the freezing waterfalls, laughing and squealing with joy. Sometimes we'd go off for long tramps up in the hills. We'd watch the eagles soaring out above the mountain tops. We'd wander the forests, always on the lookout for telltale signs of deer or wild boar, or even bears. Sometimes we might even catch a brief glimpse of one through the trees. Best of all we'd stop from time to time, just to be still, to feel the peace and breathe in the beauty. We'd listen to the sounds of the forest, to the whisper of the wind, to the cry of wolves, distant wolves I longed to see but never did.

There'd be picnics, too, with all of us there. Grandma, Mother, Father and me, and while they slept afterwards, stretched out in the sun, I'd go rolling down the hills, over and over, and end up lying there breathless on my back, giddy with happiness, the clouds and mountains spinning all about me.

I didn't like school any more than I liked church. But Mother was much more strict with me about school than she ever was about church. Father took my side in this. He always said that school and books had never done him much good, and that Mother fussed me too much. "A day in the mountains will teach him a whole lot more than a week in school," he'd say. But Mother was adamant. She never let me miss a day of it, no matter how much I complained of stomach-ache or headache. I could never fool Mother – I don't know why I went on bothering even to try. She knew me and my little games far too well. She knew I'd lie shamelessly, invent anything not to have to go into that school playground and line up with the others, not to have to face the four walls of the classroom again, not to have to face the teachers' endless questions, nor the mocking banter of my friends when I made mistakes, which I very often did. So there I'd find myself, day after day, wishing away the hours, gazing out at the mountains and forests where I so longed to be.

As soon as school was over each afternoon, I ran straight back home for my bread and honey, and then I was out to play as quick as I could. Not that I didn't like my bread and honey. I adored it. I was always so hungry after school. And besides, Mother baked the best bread in the world, and Father made the best honey, or rather his bees did. Father was a beekeeper, as well as a bit of a farmer too. We had a little farm, a few goats on the hillside, some pigs and hens in the farmyard and a couple of cows, but honey was his main business. He kept dozens of beehives all over the mountain slopes, so there was always plenty of honey. I never tired of it, especially the honeycomb, even though the waxy bits stuck in my teeth afterwards. Much less welcome was the mug of milk that Mother always forced me to drink before she let me go out to play. "Fresh from the cow," she'd say. "Good for you." Good for me or not, I hated milk with a passion. But I learnt to swallow it down fast, so fast that I hardly tasted it, knowing that the quicker I got it over with the sooner I could be up in my beloved mountains again. Sometimes I'd go off with Father, feeding the bees in winter, collecting the honey in summer. I loved that, loved being with him, doing a proper job. But although I never told him so, I much preferred to be on my own. Alone I could go where I wanted. Alone my thoughts and dreams could run free. I could sing at the top of my voice. I could soar with the eagles, be wild in the woods with the deer and the boar and bears and the invisible wolves. Alone, I could be myself.

Then one afternoon after school I was just finishing off my mug of milk when I noticed Mother putting on her coat to go out. "I need to do some shopping, Tomas. D'you want to come with me?"

"I hate shopping," I told her.

"I know you do, Tomas," she said. "That's why I thought I'd take you down to the library. It'll be something different for you. It's all miserable and wet out there today.

You don't want to be running about outside in weather like this."

"I do," I told her. But I knew she wasn't listening.

"You'll get soaked through. You'll catch your death. And anyway, you're always out there clambering around up in those

mountains. You want to watch out, you know. You go on like that and you'll grow four legs and a pair of horns, and I'll end up with a goat for a son. No, just for once you can go to the library instead. Don't worry, you won't have to come shopping with me. I'll go off and do the shopping on my own, whilst you go to the library and listen to some stories. Apparently there's this new librarian lady and she tells lovely stories. It'll be fun."

"It won't be fun," I said. "I hate stories. And anyway, stories aren't lovely. We have them at school." Already I could tell that Mother had made up her mind about this.

Already I knew this was another battle I was not going to win. Even so, I was determined to go down fighting. I was still protesting vehemently as she put on my coat. "It'll be good for you, Tomas. Everyone says this new librarian lady is really wonderful. She does it every afternoon, tells stories to any children who want to listen."

"But I don't want to listen," I protested. It didn't do me any good.

"Well you won't know that until you've heard her, will you?" By now she had me firmly by the hand and we were out of the house and hurrying down the road in the

rain. She wasn't pulling me along, exactly
– she wouldn't have done that – but I was
dragging my feet all I could, making as much
of a nuisance of myself as possible, just so
she'd know I wasn't giving in that easily, just
to show how deep was my indignation at her
outrageous infringement of my liberty. In

the end, though, and partly because people were watching, I gave up the unequal struggle and went along with her as quietly as a lamb all the way down the main street and past the Town Hall. Mother walked me up the steps and into the entrance hall of the library, took off my coat and shook it dry. "Off you go, Tomas," she said, smoothing my hair. "I'll be back for you in an hour or so, all right? Enjoy yourself. Be good." And she was gone.

Even now I still hesitated. Through the glass doors I could see there was an excited huddle of children gathering in the far corner of the library. Most of them were from my school. Frano with the sticking up hair was there, and Anna, Christina, Dani and Antonio and a dozen others. None of them were in my class. None of them were my friends at all. Every one of them was younger than me. Some were too small to come to school at all – 'little snotties' as Father always called children of that age. I absolutely did not want to be sitting and listening to stories with a bunch of 'little snotties'. I had just about decided I wasn't going to stay, that I'd leave before anyone saw I was there, that I'd run up into the hills and face Mother's fury later, when I noticed they were jostling one another as if suddenly desperate to get a better look at something. It had to be something very interesting, that was for sure, and since I could not see what it was they were all getting so frantic about, I thought I'd move a little closer. So I found myself being drawn inside the main library and walking past the

bookshelves towards this excited huddle of children in the corner.

Wanting to keep well out of sight, I half hid myself behind a bookshelf and looked on from a safe distance. As I watched, the children began to settle down, each of them finding a place to sit on the carpet. Then, quite improbably and inexplicably, they were all hushed, and still and attentive. That was the moment I first saw him, sitting there in the corner beyond the children. A unicorn! A real live unicorn! He was sitting absolutely still, his feet tucked neatly underneath him, his head turned towards us. He seemed to be gazing straight at me. I swear his eyes were smiling at me, too. He was pure white, as unicorns are, white head, body, mane and tail, white all over except for his golden horn and his little black hooves. And his eyes were blue and shining. It was some moments before I realized he was in fact not real, not live at all. He was too still to be real, his gaze was too constant and stony.

I suddenly felt very cross with myself for having been so stupid as to believe he could have been alive in the first place. Unicorns weren't actually real, I knew that much. Of course I did. It was quite obvious to me now

that this was in fact a wooden unicorn. He

had been carved out of wood and painted. But

even as I came closer he seemed so lifelike.

He looked so much how a unicorn should be,

so magical and mysterious, that if he'd got to

his feet and trotted off I still wouldn't have

been in the least surprised.

Beside the unicorn, and just as motionless,

there now stood a lady with a bright, flowery

scarf around her shoulders, her hand resting

on the unicorn's flowing mane. She must

have noticed me skulking there by the

bookshelf, still hesitant, still undecided,

because suddenly she was beckoning me to

join them. Everyone had turned to stare at me now. I decided I would make a run for it, and began to back away. "It's all right," she said. "You can come and join us if you'd like to."

So it was that I found myself moments later sitting cross-legged on the floor with the others, watching her and waiting. She was patting the unicorn and smoothing his neck. She sat down on him then, but very carefully. She was treating him as if he was real, as if she didn't want in any way to alarm him. She gentled him, brushing his forehead with the back of her hand. Her hand, like

the rest of her, was small and delicate and elegant. All around me now was the silence of expectation. No one moved. Nothing happened. No one said anything.

Suddenly the girl sitting next to me – Anna, it was – spoke up. "The unicorn story, Miss! We want the unicorn story!" Now everyone was clamouring for the same story.

"The unicorn story! The unicorn story!"

"Very well, children," said the lady, holding up her hand to quieten everyone down. "We'll begin with the unicorn story then." She paused, closed her eyes for a few moments. Then, opening them and looking straight at me, she began. "Look out of the window, children. It's raining, isn't it? Have you ever wondered what would happen if the rain never stopped? This is a story about what happened a long, long time ago when one day it started to rain, and never stopped. It just went on and on. It all began because God was very angry at the world, because he saw the world was full of wicked people who didn't care about one another, nor for the beautiful world in which they lived. They had become cruel and selfish and greedy, and God wanted to teach all of them a lesson they would never forget. He decided there was only one way to do this. He would destroy all those wicked people, but he needed to be sure that the few people that were good and kind would survive, and the animals, too – after all, the animals had never done anyone any harm, had they? This way he would be giving the world a second chance, a completely new start.

"So God chose the wisest and kindest man he could find. He was an old man called Noah. He told Noah he must build himself a great ship, a wooden ark, and he must begin it right away, and he had to make it big, the biggest ark ever built, because there had to be room not just for Noah and his family, but for two of every kind of animal on earth. So Noah and his family cut down the tallest trees. They sawed the wood into planks and began to build a huge ark, a gigantic ark, exactly as God had told him."

The lady on the unicorn was speaking so softly that I had to lean forward to hear her. I didn't want to miss a single word. "Of course," she went on, "all their neighbours thought they were barking mad to be building a ship in the middle of the countryside – off their heads, doolally. But that didn't bother Noah and his family, not one bit. They just ignored them and went right on building. It took them years and years to build such a huge ark, but finally when it was done they set about finding the animals. Two by two they brought them in, one male, one female of every kind of animal you can think of. There were lions and tigers, elephants and giraffes, cows, pigs, sheep, horses, deer, foxes, badgers, wolves and bears, wombats and wallabies – and bees and butterflies and grasshoppers too, insects of every sort. But, no matter how hard they searched they could not find any unicorns anywhere, not even one.

"Now Noah's grandchildren (and he had plenty of them) especially loved unicorns, as all children do. They spent weeks and months scouring the countryside all around looking just for unicorns. By now the rain was beginning to fall, a hard, heavy rain, a driving rain, a lashing rain, a constant rain, rain such as Noah and his family had never

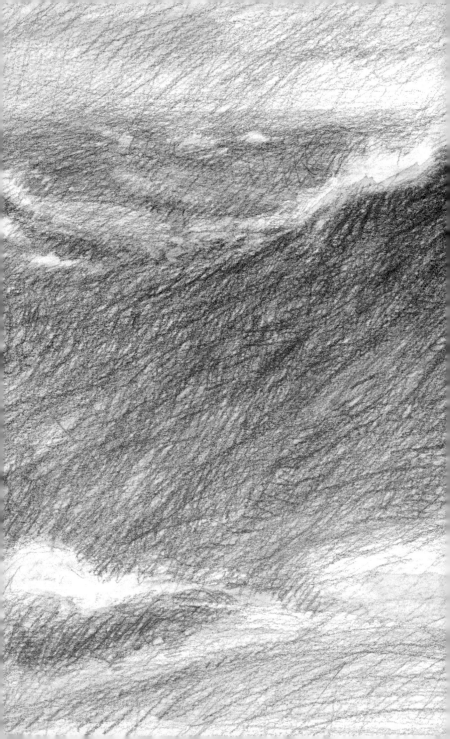

seen before. From the safety of the ark, filled now with two of every living creature on earth – except unicorns, that is – Noah and all his family looked out and saw the lakes and rivers filling, saw the land flooding about them and felt the ark begin to float beneath them. Every valley was now a rushing, roaring torrent. All the towns and villages were swept away and all the wicked people with them. Still it rained and still it rained, until all that was left of the land were a few distant mountain tops.

"Inside the ark Noah and his family might have been safe, but they were not at all happy, his grandchildren in particular. 'What about the unicorns?' they cried, time and again. 'We haven't saved the unicorns.'

"They were quite inconsolable, until Noah came up with a wonderful idea. 'Why don't I make you one?' he said. 'I'll carve it out of wood. It'll look almost the same as a real one. You'll be able to sit on it, you'll be able to ride it. And unicorns are supposed to be lucky creatures, magical creatures, aren't they? It'll bring us luck and we're going to need luck on this journey, lots of it.' So to keep the children happy Noah carved them a unicorn, and like this one, it was splendid and beautiful and magical. The children loved to play on the unicorn, and sometimes Noah himself would sit on it and tell them stories, stories they loved, stories they would never forget.

"It wasn't Noah's fault, nor his children's, nor his grandchildren's. They were all busy down below feeding the animals in the ark. They didn't see, they didn't know that high on a nearby mountain top, watching the ark drift right past them, stood the last two unicorns left alive on this earth. How they neighed and whinnied! How they reared up and pawed the air with their hooves! They tossed their heads and shook their manes, but it was no use. All too soon the ark had disappeared over the horizon. So the unicorns were left stranded on the mountain top in the wind and rain, with nothing all around them but the heaving sea. Lightning forked and flashed through the clouds. Thunder rolled and rumbled around the world. Twisting tornadoes whipped the sea into a frenzy of fury. The great flood was spreading out over all the Earth and drowning it.

"As for the poor, stranded unicorns, the waters rose and rose around them until first their hooves were covered, then their backs,

so that in the end, like it or not, they simply had to swim. They swam and they swam for hours, for days, for weeks. Then at last, at long last, the rain stopped, and the skies cleared above them. But still there was no land in sight. The unicorns swam on and on, hoping always to find land. But they never did.

"Far away and quite unbeknown to the unicorns, Noah's ark had come to rest on the top of Mount Ararat. Noah let the animals go as God had told him he should, two by two, so that once again the Earth would be filled with creatures of all kinds, from grasshoppers to giraffes. From the wood of the ark, Noah built himself a house, while his family spread out all over the world. And now all these years later, children, there are millions and millions of us, including me, and you. So in a way we're all Noah's children, if you see what I'm saying."

No one spoke for a moment or two. Then someone said, "What happened to the two unicorns, Miss?"

"I was coming to that," she replied. "Those unicorns, they swam and they swam so far, for so long, for so many years that in the end they didn't need their legs any more at all. And slowly, slowly, very slowly they turned themselves into whales. This way

they could swim more easily. This way they
could dive down to the bottom of the sea to
feed whenever they wanted, and of course
whenever they wished they could come
up for air again. But in all this time they
never lost their magical powers, and they
never lost their horns, either. Which is why

there really are to this very day whales in the sea with unicorns' horns. We call them narwhals." She leant forward, her voice dropping to a whisper. "And sometimes, children, when they've had enough of the great, wide ocean and long to see children again and hear their laughter – unicorns particularly love children because they know that children particularly love them – they swim up onto the beaches on bright moonlit nights, and become unicorns once more, wonderful, magical unicorns, like this one. So I believe in them absolutely."

For some time after she had finished no one spoke a word. It was as if we were all waking up from a dream none of us wanted to leave. There were more stories after this, and some poems, too. She had a bag of books beside her on the floor, her "special books", she called them, the ones she loved best. Sometimes she would read from these books. Sometimes she would make up stories herself, or perhaps she knew them by heart – I wasn't sure which. It was the same with any story she told, every poem she recited, I just never wanted it to end. And when she finished each one, all I wanted was more.

"Now, children," she said, closing the book she had been reading from. "Now it's your turn. Who would like to tell us a story today?"

A hand went up at once. It was Frano with the sticking up hair. "Me, Miss," he said. "Can I tell a story, Miss?" And so Frano told us a story about a duck that couldn't quack like other ducks, and could only talk instead, and how the other ducks laughed at him for being stupid, because he couldn't quack like they did. After Frano's story, there was Anna's, and then another and another. Everyone, it seemed, wanted their turn on the magical unicorn. I longed to have a try, but at the same time I was scared stiff. It wasn't just that I was frightened of making a fool of myself, I was simply terrified of being out there and talking in front of everyone. So I kept my hand down and let the others do it. The hour of stories flew by. On the way back home Mother asked me if I had enjoyed myself, if the stories had been good. "All right, I suppose," I conceded gracelessly. Well I wasn't going to give her the satisfaction, was I?

But at school the next day I told some of my friends all about the Unicorn Lady – all the little snotties seemed to call her that – and about her amazing stories and the magical storytelling powers of the unicorn. I told them they should come along and hear her for themselves. They weren't impressed. I mean stories and poems weren't exactly cool amongst my friends at school; but out of curiosity, I think, one or two of them did come along with me to the library that afternoon. As it turned out, one or two was enough, because one or two soon became a few and then a few became many. Day after day, as word spread in the school playground about the Unicorn Lady, the little group in the library grew and grew, until there was a whole crowd of us there every afternoon. We would rush out of school and race each other down the street to the library to find a spare place on the carpet as close as possible to the unicorn and the Unicorn Lady. She never once disappointed us. Every story she told, even if it was one we'd heard before, held us enthralled. It was the way she told them, I think, as if each of us was the only one she was talking to, and as if each story must be real and true, however unlikely, however fantastical. You could tell she believed absolutely in her stories as she told them. So we did, too. Each day I wanted so much to take my turn on the magical unicorn and tell everyone a story, like the others were doing. But I could never banish my fear, never summon up the courage to put up my hand.

One afternoon – and that particular afternoon I had got to the library first and was sitting in the very best place on the carpet, right beside the unicorn – the Unicorn Lady reached into her bag of "special" books and took out a book I'd never seen before. She held it up so we could all see. It looked rather old and tatty. The spine of the book was heavily taped, and the cover so stained that I found it difficult to read the title. And it was blackened too, at the edges, I noticed, as if it might have been scorched a long time ago.

"This, children," the Unicorn Lady said, "is definitely my most special book in all the world. It's my very own copy of *The Little*

Match Girl by Hans Christian Andersen. You remember him, don't you? He was the author who wrote *The Ugly Duckling*, wasn't he. And *The Snow Queen*. This book may not look much to you, but my father gave it to me when I was a young girl. So it's very special to me. Very special indeed."

"Has it been burned, Miss?" I asked.

"Yes, Tomas."

"Why Miss, what happened?"

It was a while before she answered me. I saw a shadow of sorrow come across her face, and when she spoke at last her voice trembled so much I thought she might cry.

"When I was little, even littler than any of you," she began, "I lived in another country far away from here. It was a time when wicked people ruled the land, wicked people who were frightened of the magic of stories and poems, terrified of the power of books. They knew, you see, that stories and poems help you to think and to dream. Books make you want to ask questions. And they didn't want any of us to think or dream, and especially they did not want us to ask questions. They wanted us only to think as they thought, to believe what they believed, to do as we were told. So one day in my town these wicked people went into all the bookshops and libraries and schools and brought out all the books they didn't like, which was most of them. And there in the square, soldiers in black boots and brown shirts built a huge bonfire of these books. As the books went up in flames, do you know what the soldiers did? They cheered. Can you believe that, children? They cheered. I was there with my father watching it all happen.

"Suddenly I heard my father cry out: 'No! No!' And he rushed forward and plucked a book out of the fire. He tried to beat out the flames with his bare hands. The soldiers were shouting at us, so we ran away, but they came after us and caught up with us. They knocked my father to the ground and kicked him and hit him with sticks and rifle butts. My father curled up to protect himself as best he could, but he held on to the book and would not let go, no matter how much they beat him. They tried to tear it out of his hands, but he would not let them have it. This was the book he clung on to, children, this very book. This was the book he saved. So that is why it is my favourite, most special book in all the world." As she looked down at us, the shadow seemed slowly to lift from

her, and she smiled. "And," she went on, *The Little Match Girl* also happens to be a lovely story, children; very sad but very lovely. Tomas, I wonder if you'd like to come and sit on the unicorn and read it to us. You haven't had a turn on the unicorn yet, have you?" Everyone was looking at me. They were waiting. My mouth was dry. I couldn't do it. I was filled with sudden fear. "Come on," she said. "Come and sit beside me on the unicorn."

I had never been any good at reading out loud at school. I would forever stutter over my consonants – I dreaded k's in particular.

Long words terrified me in case I pronounced them wrongly and everyone laughed at me. But now, sitting up there on the magic unicorn, I began to read, and all my dread and all my terror simply vanished. I heard my voice speaking out strong and loud. It was as if I was up in the mountains alone and singing a song at the top of my voice, for the sheer joy of the sound of it. The words danced like music on the air, and I could feel everyone listening. And I knew they were listening not to me at all, but to the story of *The Little Match Girl*, because they were just as lost in it as I was.

That same day I borrowed my first book from the library. I chose *Aesop's Fables* because I liked the animals in them, and because the Unicorn Lady had read them to us and I had loved them. I read them aloud to Mother that night when she came up to say goodnight to me. I read to her instead of her reading to me. It was the first time I'd ever done that. Father came and listened at the doorway whilst I was reading. He clapped when I'd finished. "Magic, Tomas," he said. "That was magic." There were tears in his eyes. I hoped it was because he was proud of me. How I loved him being proud of me. And Mother hugged me harder that night than she'd ever hugged me before. She could hardly speak she was so amazed. How I loved amazing Mother.

Then early one summer morning, war came to our valley. Before that morning I had known something of the war. But I didn't know what it meant, nor even why it was happening. I knew that some of the men from the town had gone to fight – Ivan Zec, the postman, Pavo Batina from the farm next to us, Tonio Raguz, Frano's brother – but I wasn't sure what for, nor where they had gone. For some time, on the television I had seen soldiers riding through the streets on tanks, waving and smiling as they roared past, giving the thumbs up. I had asked Mother about it, and she told me that it was all far, far away down south, and I wasn't to worry myself, and besides, it would be over very soon. And on one of our long walks in the forest Father had told me that we would win in the end anyway and he promised me that war would never come to our town.

I remember the very moment it did come.

I was having my breakfast with sleep still in my head. It was going to be a school day, an ordinary school day. As usual Mother was hassling me to hurry up and finish. Then as usual she sent me outside to open up the hens and feed them. We had a broody hen and I was just reaching in under her to see if her chicks had hatched out, when I heard the sound of a plane flying very low. I came out of the henhouse and saw it skimming over the rooftops. As I watched, it climbed, banked and came in again, glinting in the sunlight. It was very beautiful, like a huge, shining eagle, I thought. That was when the bombs began to fall, far away at first beyond the river, then closer, closer. Everything happened at once. Mother came running out of the house. Father had me by the hand. They were shouting at one another about who should fetch Grandma. Mother was screaming at us both to go, that she would go into town to find her. Then Father and I were running out across the fields and up into the woods. Here we stayed hidden under the trees and watched as the plane circled above us, as people came streaming out of town in their hundreds to join us in the

woods. All the while we were hoping and
hoping to see Mother and Grandma amongst
them. But they didn't come and they didn't
come. The plane dropped no more bombs
now, but buzzed over the town several times
before soaring up over the mountains and
away. When at long last we saw Mother

and Grandma hurrying towards us over the fields, we were so relieved, so happy. We ran out from under the trees to help them. Back in the shelter of the forest we huddled together, all of us, arms around one another, our foreheads pressed together, Grandma praying out loud. Mother was rocking back and forth, not crying, but moaning, as if she was in pain. I was too frightened to cry, I think. That was when Father told us we had to promise to stay where we were until he came back to fetch us. He wasn't alone. There were a few other men with him. I watched them springing down the hillside towards the town. "Where's he going?" I asked. But Mother didn't answer me. She and Grandma were both on their knees now, their lips moving in silent prayer.

We did as Father had told us and stayed where we were. So we saw it all. Hidden high up in the forest, we could see the tanks and soldiers moving through the streets blasting and shooting as they came. There were fires burning now all over the town, so many that soon we could hardly see the houses for the smoke. Then came the silence. Had they gone? Was it over? I prayed then too. Please God let it be over. Please God don't let the soldiers come back. Please God keep Father safe. For long hours we all stayed where we were with the town burning below us, unsure what to do next.

When at last we did see one of the men running towards us up the hillside, it was not my father but Frano's father. When he'd got his breath back he told us that the soldiers and tanks had all gone, that it was safe to go back home. "Where's Father?" I asked him.

"I don't know, Tomas," he said. "I haven't seen him."

Mother had to help Grandma down the hill, so I ran on ahead of them. I looked for Father at home, I called for him everywhere, but I couldn't find him. In the farmyard I found both our cows lying dead, the pigs, too. There was blood, so much blood. The house itself had not been damaged, but there was terrible destruction all around me as I ran on into town searching for Father.

I asked everyone I met if they had seen him, but no one had. Everyone was crying, and I was crying now because I couldn't forget the terrible sight of the cows and the pigs and the blood. Most of all I was beginning to fear the worst, that Father was dead and I'd never see him again.

The centre of the town had suffered the worst damage. There was hardly a building that hadn't been hit. The Town Hall was in flames, and every car in the streets was a blackened shell, some with the tyres still burning. There were men and women rushing everywhere trying to put out the fires,

with hoses, with buckets, but Father wasn't amongst them. Others simply stood dazed in the streets looking about them. Some of them could hardly speak when I asked them about Father. Old Mr Liban just shook his head and wept.

And then I saw the library. There were
flames licking out of the upper windows.
The fire engine was in the street, the
firefighters running out the hoses. "Have
you seen my father?" I asked them. "Have
you seen my father?"

But before they could answer, I saw him for myself, Father and the Unicorn Lady at the same moment. They were coming out of the library, their arms piled high with books. "I couldn't find you!" I cried, running to him. "I thought you were dead." I helped them set the books down on the steps. Father put his arms around me then, and I held him as tightly as he was holding me.

The Unicorn Lady was gazing up at the burning building. "We must go back for more," she breathed, "I won't let them burn the books. I won't."

When Father went with her back up the

steps, I tried to go too. "No, Tomas," Father told me. "You stay here and look after the books we bring out." Then both of them were running up the steps into the library, only to reappear a couple of minutes later, their arms full of books again. A crowd was beginning to gather in the square.

"We need help!" cried the Unicorn Lady. "We have to save the books."

That was the moment the great book rescue began. Suddenly there were dozens of people surging past me into the library. The firefighters warned that it was dangerous, but no one paid them any attention. It wasn't long before a whole book evacuation system had been set up. We children were organized into two human chains across the square, from the library itself to the café opposite, and all the rescued books went from hand to hand along the chains, ending up piled in great stacks all over the floor of the café and on the tables, too. When there was no more room in the café we used Mrs Danic's grocer's shop, and I remember Mrs Danic gave us free sweets because we were all working so hard.

But the moment came when the fire-fighters at last had to put a stop to it all, and wouldn't let anyone else in to fetch out any more books. The ceilings could come down at any time, they said. "The unicorn!" I cried. "What about the unicorn?" I needn't have worried. The last to emerge, faces smudged and smeared, eyes reddened, were the Unicorn Lady and Father, carrying the unicorn between them. He was blackened and burnt on his back and his legs, and his tail was missing. But his face was still white and his horn still gold. They were staggering under his weight, so I dashed up the steps to help them. As we came down together everyone began applauding, and I knew the applause was for the unicorn as much as it

was for us. The Unicorn Lady sat herself down on the unicorn, choking so much she could hardly breathe. Mrs Danic brought her a glass of water. We children anxiously gathered all around her, waiting for her to recover, waiting for her to speak. We were waiting for a story, too, I think.

"I never told you this until now, children," she began, still coughing from time to time, her voice hoarse. "But my father carved this unicorn for me when I was little. He always said it was every bit as magical as a real unicorn. So I always thought it was too, but now I know it for sure. The unicorn did it for us, children – protected the books in the library while the fire burned all around him. It was he that stayed with them, he that saved them." She smiled at us. "With a little help from his friends, of course."

She looked up at the library, at the fire now raging freely. "Don't worry, children. We'll repair the unicorn, make him white again. As for the library, it's just a building. Buildings they can destroy. Dreams they cannot. Buildings you can always build again, and we shall build our library again just as it was, maybe better. Meanwhile we shall just have to find a way to look after all the wonderful books we have saved, won't we?"

"What about in my house?" said Frano. "We could keep some of them in my house."

"And mine!" It was Anna this time.

"What a wonderful idea!" said the Unicorn Lady. "That's how we'll do it then. All of us who would like to can take away as many books as we can manage, and care for them. They must be kept dry, mind, and clean – and loved. Loved is very important. And when in one year or two or three this war is over and done with, when we have our new library again, then we can all bring back our books, and we'll carry the unicorn inside, and tell our stories once more. In the meantime we'll just have to find somewhere else to tell our stories, won't we?" She leant forward so that we all listened even more carefully. "All we have to do, children, is to make sure this story comes true. You really have to believe something will happen before you can make it happen. And we will make it happen, because I told you this story sitting on the magical unicorn, didn't I?"

So it all turned out just as the Unicorn Lady said it would. That evening every family that still had a roof over its head took home a wheelbarrow full of books and looked after them. And there were people to look after too, of course, people who had lost their houses, lost everything. Everyone was found a home somewhere. We had Frano and his family with us on our farm until they could rebuild their own place. It was a bit of a squash. I had to share my room with Frano and our pile of books. The books were fine, but Frano snored, which wasn't so fine.

The dark days of war did come to an end, and in time every house was rebuilt, and so was the library. It looked just the same as the old one, only newer, of course. The unicorn was restored and repainted, and we all brought our books back and filled the library again. So the Unicorn Lady's story came true, just as she'd said it would.

The day the new library was officially opened – and because, I suppose, Father and I had helped the Unicorn Lady to carry the unicorn out on that dreadful day – they asked all three of us to carry it back in again. The flags were flying, the band was playing. Everyone was cheering and clapping. Mother and Grandma were there too. They both cried, I noticed, and I loved that. The Mayor made a speech which began: "This is the Day of the Unicorn, the greatest day our town has known, the day we can all make a new start together." There were fireworks that evening, and singing and dancing. It was the proudest, happiest day of my life.

Now, all these years later, we have peace again in our country. We were lucky. Unlike other towns we did not lose too many people. Only Ivan Zec, the postman, didn't come home again after the war. He died in a prison camp somewhere. And Frano's brother Tonio came back blind, with one leg missing. So all is not the same again. The truth is that after war nothing is ever the same again. But the Unicorn Lady still works in the town library, still reads her stories to the children after school. I do it too, from time to time, when she asks me to, because I'm a writer now, a weaver of tales. And if from time to time I lose the thread of my story, I just go and sit on the magical unicorn in the library, and my story flows again.

So I believe in unicorns.
I believe in them absolutely.

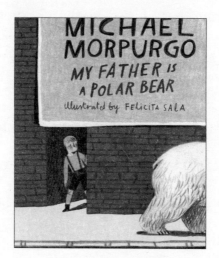

When Andrew's brother points to a photo
of a man in a bear costume and identifies him
as the father they have never met, the little
boy doesn't know what to think.

His father is a *polar bear*…?

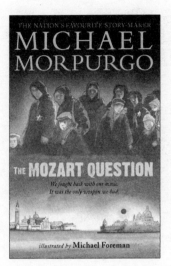

When cub reporter Lesley is sent to Venice
to interview a world-renowned violinist,
the journalist is told she can ask Paolo
Levi anything about his life and career as a
musician, but on no account must she ask
him the Mozart question; never the Mozart
question. Paolo, however, has realized he
must finally reveal the truth.

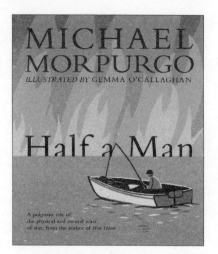

MICHAEL
MORPURGO
ILLUSTRATED BY GEMMA O'CALLAGHAN

Half a Man

A poignant tale of
the physical and mental scars
of war, from the author of *War Horse*

Michael is fascinated by and afraid of his
grandfather in equal measure, with his
disfigured, unsmiling face and taciturn
manner. Then a summer spent on the Isles
of Scilly enables him to finally see the man
behind the burns – and gives Michael the
power to heal wounds that have divided
his family for so long.

MICHAEL
MORPURGO
THE KITES ARE FLYING!
ILLUSTRATED BY LAURA CARLIN

FRIENDSHIP KNOWS NO BARRIERS

Journalist Max and his new friend Said sit
together under an ancient olive tree while
Said makes another of his kites. Max is
welcomed as a guest in the boy's home, and
learns of the terrible events in his family's
past – but nothing prepares him for the true
importance of Said's kites. A beautiful tale
of tragedy and hope that rings with joy.

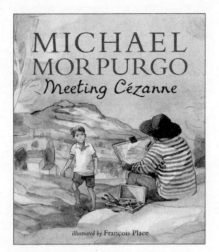

MICHAEL
MORPURGO
Meeting Cézanne

illustrated by François Place

Many images from that spring in the
south of France will stay with Yannick:
his kind, jolly aunt and uncle; his beautiful
green-eyed cousin Amandine; the dark
pointing trees and gentle hills so beloved of
his mother's hero, the painter Cézanne.
And as Provence weaves its magic over the
young boy, a part of him is changed for ever.

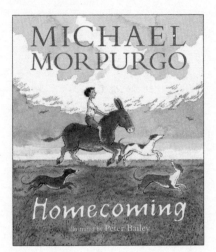

Michael loves to visit Mrs Pettigrew in her
railway carriage by the sea, where she lives
with her donkey, dogs and hens. But when
plans are made to build a nuclear power
station, Mrs Pettigrew's idyllic life becomes
threatened and Michael learns that
nothing can ever stay the same.

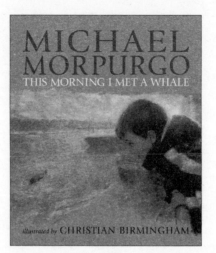

At sunrise, young Michael spots a whale on
the shores of the Thames and thinks he
must be dreaming. But the creature is real
and brings a message for him – humans
must mend the damage they are doing to
the planet before it is too late. Can he fulfil
his promise to tell others when neither his
teacher nor his classmates believe his story?

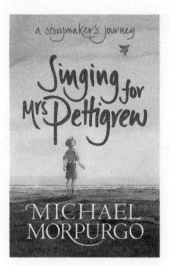

A wonderful and unique collection of
stories and the story of their making;
an engaging insight into the craft of one
of today's most loved storytellers.

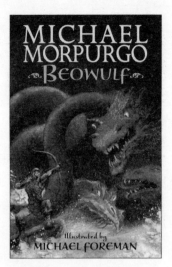

"Hear and listen well, and I will tell you
a tale that has been told for a thousand years
and more. It may be an old story, yet it
troubles and terrifies us now as much as it
ever did, for we still fear the evil that stalks
out there in the darkness and beyond."

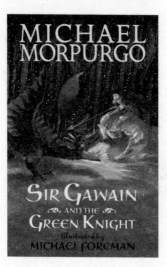

"My story is of Gawain.
Of all the tales of the knights of the
round table, his is the most magical
and the one I most love to tell."

Michael Morpurgo was 2003–2005 Children's Laureate, has written over one hundred books and is the winner of numerous awards, including the Whitbread Children's Book Award, the Blue Peter Book Award, the Smarties Book Prize and the Red House Children's Book Award. His books are translated and read around the world and his hugely popular novel *War Horse*, already a critically acclaimed stage play, is now also a blockbuster film. Michael and his wife, Clare, founded the charity Farms for City Children and live in Devon.

Gary Blythe has illustrated many books for children, including *The Whales' Song*, written by Dyan Sheldon, for which he won the Kate Greenaway Medal; *Ice Bear* by Nicola Davies; and *Bram Stoker's Dracula*, retold by Jan Needle. Gary lives in the Wirral, near Liverpool.